Catherine
the Fashion Princess
Fairy

FOR SALE
WITHDRAWN
FROM STOCK

D0177052

Special thanks to
Rachel Elliot

ORCHARD BOOKS
Carmelite House, 50 Victoria Embankment, London EC4Y 0DZ
Orchard Books Australia
Level 17/207 Kent Street, Sydney, NSW 2000
A Paperback Original

First published in 2015 by Orchard Books

HiT entertainment

A CIP catalogue record for this book is available
from the British Library.

ISBN 978 1 40833 946 6

1 3 5 7 9 10 8 6 4 2

Printed and bound by CPI Group (UK) Ltd, Croydon, CR0 4YY

MIX
Paper from
responsible sources
FSC® C104740
www.fsc.org

The paper and board used in this book are made from wood from responsible sources

Orchard Books is an imprint of Hachette Children's Group and published by the Watts
Publishing Group Limited, an Hachette UK company.

www.hachette.co.uk

Catherine
the Fashion Princess
Fairy

by Daisy Meadows

ORCHARD

www.rainbowmagic.co.uk

Jack Frost's Ice Castle

Throne Room

Grand City Gallery

The Yellow Room

Jack Frost's Spell

Princesses live a life of ease,
With clever servants, keen to please.
My life should be this grand and fine,
So Catherine's objects must be mine!

I want applause for how I dress.
I want my speeches to impress.
Goblins, take her objects three,
And give her regal flair to me!

The Priceless Earring

Contents

The
Palace Gates

"Three cheers for the princesses!" shouted
an excited tourist.

Outside the royal gates, Rachel Walker
and Kirsty Tate cheered along with the
rest of the crowd, and then gazed up
at the palace in the heart of the city.
The elegant, spiral bars were painted
gold, and decorated with tiny silver
hummingbirds.

"Isn't it amazing to think that your mum's friend is in there right now, talking to the youngest princess?" said Rachel to her best friend.

Kirsty nodded. Everyone loved the three princesses, but the youngest – Princess Edie – was their favourite.

"I wonder which room is hers," she said.

"I think it's that one," said Rachel, pointing up at an open window where white curtains were billowing in the summer breeze.

"Bee has such a different life from us," said Kirsty.

"I can't imagine what it must be like to be a fashion stylist and help a princess decide what to wear every day!"

"Her house is amazing too," Rachel added. "I wonder what it's like to live in the city."

"We're going to find out this weekend," said Kirsty with a grin.

Rachel and Kirsty were visiting the city for the weekend with Kirsty's parents. They were staying with Bee, who was an old friend of Kirsty's mother from university.

"Bee always has such interesting stories to tell about the princesses," Kirsty went on. "It's so much fun hearing about what their lives are like. She loves Princess Edie best of all."

"I wish she'd hurry up," said Rachel, gazing up at the window with the billowing curtains. "I can't wait to start sightseeing. I want to visit all the most famous places in the city."

The girls were waiting with Kirsty's parents to meet Bee when she had

finished in the palace. Mr and Mrs
Tate were taking photos of the sentry
guard, and Kirsty slipped her arm
through Rachel's.

"It's very different from the palace
in Fairyland, isn't it?" she said in a
soft voice.

Rachel smiled, thinking of the beautiful pink palace where Queen Titania and King Oberon lived. They had been friends of Fairyland ever since they first met on Rainspell Island, and they loved sharing their magical secret.

"It's exciting being here," said Rachel. "But I hope that we get to see the Fairyland Palace again soon."

"You may see it sooner than you think," said a silvery voice.

The girls jumped in surprise, and then stepped closer to the gate. An exquisitely dressed fairy was standing with her arm around one of the spiral bars.

Fashion in the Tower

The little fairy was wearing a flowing dress of green chiffon, with a sparkling belt clasp and delicate lacy sleeves. A tiny pillbox hat was perched at an angle on her head, and her glossy brown hair coiled over her shoulder.

"Hello," she said. "I'm Catherine the Fashion Princess Fairy."

"Hello, Catherine," whispered Kirsty, glancing around to check that her parents weren't watching. "What are you doing here at the palace?"

"I've come to find you," said Catherine, her eyes sparkling as she looked at them. "There's a problem in Fairyland – please will you come and help?"

"Of course we will," said Rachel at

once. "But Catherine, we're at the palace! It's one of the busiest places in the whole city – there are people everywhere. How can we be magicked away to Fairyland right under their noses?"

Kirsty turned her head and gazed at all the eager tourists, snapping photographs, pointing at the palace, laughing and joking. Then she looked in the other direction and smiled.

"I've got an idea," she said, pointing to a large postbox at the corner of the

palace fence. "Let's slip behind there. It's so big that we'll be hidden from sight."

Catherine fluttered into Rachel's backpack. Mr and Mrs Tate were poring over a guidebook, and they didn't notice the girls darting over to the postbox and ducking out of sight behind it. Catherine peeped out of the backpack and raised her wand.

"Are you ready?" she asked the girls.

"Ready for another adventure?" said Kirsty. "Always!"

As Catherine flourished her wand, the area behind the postbox was hidden in a haze of emerald-green sparkles. Rachel and Kirsty felt gauzy wings appear on their backs, and they fluttered them in delight as they shrank to fairy size. A ribbon of green sparkles coiled around them, dazzling them, and they closed their eyes.

"Welcome to my dressing room," said Catherine's soft voice.

23

A sweet fragrance filled the air, and the girls slowly opened their eyes. They were standing between long racks filled with silk gowns, satin cloaks and net skirts. Towers of jewelled shoes spun slowly, and tiaras, bracelets and diamond pendants sparkled in velvet trays.

Sunshine was pouring through an arched window, and Rachel and Kirsty

went over to look outside.

"We're in the Fairyland Palace!"
Rachel exclaimed.

"Yes, we're inside one of the towers,"
said Catherine. "This is the chamber
where I keep my fashion collection."

"It's incredible," said Kirsty,
gazing at rows of feather
boas and strings of pearls.

"I've never seen so many dresses."

"And shoes, and scarves, and bags, and hats!" Rachel went on, darting around the chamber in delight.

"It's my job to make sure that princesses everywhere look fabulous and behave perfectly at all their royal functions," Catherine went on.

"I expect you're brilliant at that," said Kirsty.

"I'm not so sure," said Catherine in a sad voice. "Princess Grace is going to make an important speech in a few days.

She's relying on me to help her look and sound her best. But this morning, someone broke into this chamber and stole my most precious belongings!"

Silken Clues

Rachel and Kirsty each took one of Catherine's hands.

"Tell us what happened," said Rachel. "We'll help you if we can."

"Queen Titania tried to find out what had happened in her Seeing Pool," Catherine told them. "She saw that some goblins had crept in here and taken my three objects."

"That means Jack Frost must be behind it," said Kirsty. "The goblins are naughty, but they wouldn't have planned that all by themselves. Where did they take them?"

"The queen wasn't able to see," said Catherine. "All we know is they took the objects and walked out of the chamber. After that, it's a mystery."

"What are the objects?" Rachel asked.

Catherine led them over to a gilded dressing table with three drawers in it.

"The priceless earring belongs in the first drawer," she said, showing them that it was empty. "It makes sure that every princess teams a beautiful outfit with the perfect accessories. It was a gift from Shannon the Ocean Fairy."

She opened the second drawer, which was also empty.

"This is where the sparkling ornamental shoe should be," she went on. "It was a gift from Lucy the Diamond Fairy, and it makes sure that princesses are always on time for their royal functions."

31

Kirsty opened the third drawer.

"What belongs in here?" she asked.

"Claudia the Accessories Fairy gave me the jewelled clutch bag," Catherine said. "It gives princesses the confidence to make wonderful speeches."

Rachel frowned. "What will happen if Jack Frost and his goblins keep the magical objects?"

Catherine closed the third drawer and her head drooped.

"Until the objects are back in their drawers, Jack Frost will possess all my fashion princess magic," she said. "Fashion disasters will strike the human and fairy worlds, and all royal events will be at risk."

Rachel sat down on a plush velvet chair and looked around the chamber.

"Then we must find them as fast as we can," she said. "How did the goblins manage to get in?"

"Good question," said Catherine, perching beside her on the arm of the chair. "Bertram the footman didn't see anyone come in from the main entrance, and Jack Frost's magic isn't strong enough to allow him to magic the goblins inside the castle."

"If they didn't come up from the main entrance, they must have somehow come

down from the turret," said Kirsty. "Let's go up and see if we can figure out how they got in."

"How will that help us?" asked Catherine.

"I don't know," said Rachel, jumping to her feet. "But we have to start somewhere!"

The three fairies left the chamber and fluttered up a narrow staircase to the turret. Blinking in the bright sunshine, at first they found it hard to see anything.

Then Kirsty gave a shout of excitement.

"Look!" she cried, pouncing on something that was lying on the floor.

"What is it?" asked Rachel.

Kirsty held up three large pieces of green material.

"What strange clothes," said Catherine.

"These aren't clothes," said Rachel, looking closely at the material. "These are parachutes. That's how the goblins got in!"

"But how did they get out?" asked Catherine.

Kirsty gave a

36

sudden exclamation.

"Oh my goodness," she cried. "Maybe they're still in the palace!"

Hunt the Goblins

"Let's go and ask Bertram if he's seen anything," said Catherine.

Although they were worried for Catherine, the girls felt excited as they flew down to find the frog footman. Bertram had taken part in several of their adventures and was a loyal and faithful friend.

"Kirsty! Rachel!" he said when they found him in the entrance hall. "How delightful to welcome you to the palace again."

"It's good to see you too, Bertram," said Rachel, giving him a hug. "Listen, we think that the goblins who took Catherine's belongings might still be somewhere in the palace. Have you seen anything strange?"

"I haven't seen anything," said Bertram, shaking his head with a solemn air.

"Then we will have to search the palace," said Kirsty, looking around. "It seems very quiet here today."

"The fairies have gone for a picnic in the bluebell forest," said Bertram. "The queen and the king are strolling in the garden."

Catherine, Kirsty and Rachel exchanged determined glances.

"Then it's up to us," said Rachel. "We'll

have to search the
palace from
top to bottom
until we find
those goblins.
If we're
lucky, we
might find the
objects before
the goblins even
leave these walls."

It was strange to see all the rooms
empty. The fairies fluttered from chamber
to chamber, searching for any sign of the
mischievous goblins. But there was no
sound and no disturbance – everything
was peaceful.

Back in the entrance hall, the fairies
stared at each other.

"Let's go up the main staircase and search the next floor," said Catherine.

Kirsty nodded, but Rachel shook her head and put her finger to her lips.

"Shh, listen!" she whispered.

Muffled squawks and giggles were coming from the small cloakroom at the side of the entrance hall. As gracefully as a ballerina, Catherine tiptoed towards the door, followed by Rachel and Kirsty. Together, they pushed the door open as slowly as they could.

Inside, three goblins were prancing

43

around in front of a large silver mirror. Catherine drew in her breath sharply.

"They're wearing my magical objects!" she whispered. "Look!"

Peering over her shoulder, Rachel and Kirsty saw that one goblin had a pearl earring dangling from his large left ear. Another was holding up a glittering ornamental shoe, and the third had a jewel-studded clutch bag tucked under his arm.

"I look so elegant," said the first, shaking his head so that the earring swung round and hit the second goblin on the nose.

"You clumsy nincompoop!" squealed the second goblin.

The third goblin used the clutch bag to bash the other two over the head and

giggled. Furious,
Rachel let out an
indignant cry
and flung the
door wide open.

"Scarper!" the
goblins shouted,
diving for the
open window.

"Stop them!"
exclaimed Kirsty.

The fairies darted across
the room, but two of the goblins had
already managed to claw their way out
of the window. The third was halfway
out, his large feet scrabbling against the
wall.

"Not so fast!" cried Rachel, grabbing
one leg.

"Come back!" said Kirsty, seizing the other leg.

As the goblin slid back into the room, Catherine leaned towards him and

unclipped the earring from his ear.

"You rotten fairies!" he said, scowling. "You'll be sorry for this!"

"This magical earring belongs to me,"

said Catherine
in a gentle
voice.

The
goblin
shook his
fist at her
and then
stuck out
his tongue.

"You'll be sorry!"
he screeched angrily.
"Anyway, it doesn't matter.
Jack Frost will still have the shoe and the
bag. We're going to hide them and you'll
never guess where!"

The goblin gave a sharp kick of
his legs, and Kirsty and Rachel were
suddenly flung backwards. Before the

girls and Catherine could stop him, he
had hurled himself out of the window
and was gone.

A Solemn Promise

Catherine held the earring tightly in her hand as Bertram appeared in the doorway, puffing and holding his tummy.

"Are you all right?" he exclaimed. "I heard squawking!"

"That was the goblins," said Rachel.

"You found the objects?" asked

Bertram, a smile spreading over his face. "Well done."

"Not all of them," said Kirsty, staring at the window through which the goblins had escaped.

"But do I have my pearl earring back," said Catherine, holding it up in delight. "Thanks to Rachel and Kirsty, princesses in both the human and fairy worlds will be able to find the perfect outfits again."

"I just wish we had been able to get all

three of your objects back," said Rachel.

"We'll find the other two," said Kirsty, putting her arm around Catherine's shoulders. "We won't give up until they are all back in their drawers – we promise."

Catherine gave them a dazzling smile.

"Thank you," she said. "It makes me feel so much happier to know that you are helping me. But for now, it's time for you to return to the human world."

She flicked her wand and the scene around them started to blur. The last thing they saw was Bertram waving,

and then they
were standing
behind the
red postbox,
human-
sized again.

"There
you are,
girls," said
Mrs Tate as
they stepped
out from behind
the postbox. "I'm
sorry about the wait. Bee was supposed
to be here twenty minutes ago."

Rachel and Kirsty looked at each
other.

"I wonder where the goblins have
taken the ornamental shoe," said Rachel.

"And the jewelled clutch bag," said Kirsty in a low voice.

"I hope we can find out in time for Princess Grace's speech," said Rachel. "Jack Frost is so mean to want to spoil things for princesses everywhere."

"Did someone mention princesses?" asked a merry voice.

It was Bee, looking as stylish as always with her sleek black bob and simple dress. She hugged them all and apologised for being late.

"Everything went wrong when I was dressing Princess Edie today," she said.

"Nothing seemed to suit her or fit, and I couldn't find any accessories to match. But then, at the last minute, the whole outfit came together and the princess was happy."

"It sounds very stressful," said Mrs Tate, sounding sympathetic.

"I just hope that the same thing doesn't happen tomorrow," Bee went on. "The princess is going to the opening of a new gallery and she'll need a special outfit."

"Thank goodness we found the earring in time!" Rachel whispered to Kirsty.

"No more delays," said Bee, clapping her hands together. "Time for a grand afternoon out in the city!"

Rachel and Kirsty shared excited smiles. They knew that they had two more objects to get back from Jack Frost and his goblins, but right now they had a city to explore!

The Ornamental Shoe

Contents

A Royal Surprise

Rachel opened her eyes and smiled. The sound of birdsong drifted through the open window, and the sun was shining though the curtains.

"I can see why Bee calls it the Yellow Room," she said.

Kirsty sat up in bed and looked around. The curtains were yellow, the wallpaper was decorated with daffodils and there was a vase of miniature sunflowers on the dressing table.

"It must feel like summertime all year round in here," said Kirsty.

Rachel jumped out of bed and went to gaze out of the window. Bee's house overlooked a park, where a few early risers were already jogging or walking their dogs. The rooftops and towers of the city glittered in the distance.

"I'm glad it really *is* summertime at the moment," she said.

"It's great fun visiting the city when the sun is shining."

"I wonder what we're doing today," said Kirsty as the bedroom door opened and Mrs Tate bustled in.

"I'll tell you what we're doing, girls," she said. "Bee has surprised us with tickets for a very special royal gallery opening, so hurry up and get dressed. We're going to meet Princess Edie!"

"*Really?*" Kirsty exclaimed, leaping out of bed. "That's amazing, Mum!"

Bee popped her head around the door and grinned at them.

"You've heard about my little surprise, then?" she asked.

"Thank you so much!" said Rachel, darting over to give her a hug. "Princess Edie is our favourite!"

"I've got something for you both," said
Bee.

She gave each of the girls a purple
velvet purse.

"Princess Edie has
one of these,"
she said. "She
loves it, and I
was sure you
would too."

"Thank
you!" said
Rachel and
Kirsty together.

Princess Edie
always had lovely
clothes and accessories, so it was exciting
for the girls to know that they had the
same purse. They quickly got dressed

and had breakfast. Then they all walked to the nearest bus stop. Lots of buses whizzed by, all with different numbers.

"Here's ours," said Bee at last.

"I'm glad we're here with Bee," said Mrs Tate as they climbed onto the bus. "All these different bus numbers are so confusing."

"It doesn't take long to get used to it when you live here," said Bee with a smile.

"It must be such an exciting place to live," Rachel said.

"I like living in Wetherbury best," said Kirsty. "But visiting the city is great fun!"

Soon they were walking in between the grand entrance pillars. The reception hall was filled with important-looking people, all wearing their best clothes. A small group of schoolchildren was standing in the centre, all looking very impressed. Waiters and waitresses were carrying silver trays of drinks around.

"Look at the wall over there," said Bee to the girls.

She pointed to a small red curtain on the wall, with a gold tassel hanging beside it.

"What's that for?" asked Kirsty.

"There's a special plaque behind it," Bee explained. "The princess will draw the curtain and declare the gallery officially open."

"I wonder if she's here yet," Rachel said, gazing around.

"Not yet," said Bee. "When she arrives, everyone will line up to meet her and shake her hand."

"This is so exciting," said Mrs Tate. "I suppose you've been to lots of these occasions, Bee?"

Bee nodded.

"I still get excited though," she said. "And it is fun to see the princess wearing an outfit that I chose for her."

While Kirsty's parents chatted to Bee, the girls went to have a closer look at the curtain. Rachel lifted the tassel to feel how heavy it was, and the curtain moved.

"You shouldn't pull that," said Kirsty. "Someone will tell us off."

"I didn't!" Rachel replied, letting go of the tassel. "Look — it's still moving!"

As they stared at the curtain, Catherine the Fashion Princess Fairy's head popped out over the top of it!

A Naughty School Group

"Catherine!" said Kirsty in an excited whisper. "Quickly – hide in my purse!"

She unclasped her tiara purse and Catherine fluttered into it. The girls went and stood in a quiet corner so they could talk to her.

"I'm so glad I've found you," she said.

"Jack Frost has been boasting that he's
hidden my other two objects here in the
human world. Please, will you help me
look for them?"

The girls looked at each other.

"Of course we'll help you," said Rachel
at once. "But we really want to watch
the gallery opening as well. Could we
wait to see the princess?"

"Oh yes!" said Catherine at once. "I

know all about the opening ceremony. I'm looking forward to seeing Princess Edie too. I just hope that everything goes smoothly. After all, while the ornamental shoe and the jewelled clutch bag are still missing, things could go terribly wrong with any royal visit."

Just then, the chatter of the crowd died down, and then a tense whisper rippled around the room. The girls turned around and saw a worried-looking man hurrying to stand beside the curtain.

"Ahem, excuse me, ladies and gentlemen," he said in a shaky voice.

"I'm very sorry to announce that Princess Edie has been delayed, but … er … I'm sure she'll be here very soon."

The chatter started up again, louder than before. People didn't look too worried – just curious about what could have delayed the princess. But Rachel and Kirsty were alarmed.

"This is all because of Jack Frost, isn't it?" Kirsty asked.

Catherine nodded. "It's because the ornamental shoe is missing," she explained. "Without it, no princess will ever be on time for a royal function again!"

People were starting to get restless. The school group that the girls had noticed earlier was making a lot of noise. Some of the boys began to jostle each other, giggling and messing around.

"Get off!" one of the boys shouted.

"You idiot!" another one replied.

"Those boys are being really rude," said Rachel. "Why isn't their teacher telling them off?"

Just then, the teacher started walking towards the boys, and they darted away. The girls expected the teacher to follow them, but he just shook his head and turned back to the other students.

"Perhaps they're not part of his group after all," said Kirsty. "Look, their uniforms aren't quite the same. They're wearing caps, but all of the others have bare heads."

The friends stared at the boys as they scampered towards a door at the far end of the hall. It had a clear sign saying 'No Entry', but the first boy opened it and slipped out of sight. The second boy glanced around as if to check that no one was following him.

"Hey, he's got a green nose!" Rachel exclaimed.

"And beady eyes," Kirsty added. "That's a goblin!"

Through the Keyhole

"Whatever the goblins are up to, it won't be anything good," said Catherine. "What shall we do?"

"There's only one thing we *can* do," said Rachel. "We have to follow them and find out what they're doing here. We can't let them spoil the gallery opening."

"But how can we slip away?" asked

Kirsty. "Mum and Dad are sure to notice and stop us from going."

"Find a place to hide," Catherine said in a determined voice. "I'll turn you into fairies and then we'll be able to get away without being spotted. I'm not going to allow Princess  Edie's special event to be spoiled by Jack Frost's goblins!"

The girls looked at Mr and Mrs Tate. They were still talking to Bee, so if Rachel and Kirsty were going to slip out of sight, this was the moment to choose. Kirsty spotted a table filled with glasses.

The waiters and waitresses were filling up their trays from the table. It was covered with a large white tablecloth that almost reached all the way to the floor.

"How about hiding under that table?" she suggested.

"Good thinking!" said Rachel.

They hurried over and waited for a moment when no one was looking. Then they slipped under the draped cloth. It was dark, but Catherine's wand

seemed to twinkle as she waved it in the half-light. Glimmering fairy dust floated around the girls, and they smiled at each other as they changed from human girls into tiny fairies with pearly wings.

When they were Catherine's size, she hugged them tightly.

"I'm so happy to have your help," she said. "Come on, let's catch up with those naughty goblins."

Swooping under the folds of the tablecloth, the girls followed the Fashion Princess Fairy as she flew up above the heads of the other guests towards the door the goblins had gone through. Kirsty hovered above her parents for a moment, before diving  after Rachel and Catherine. But when they reached the door, they found that it was tightly shut.

"What are we going to do?" asked Catherine with panic in her voice. "We mustn't let them get away! What if they can lead me to my magical objects?"

"Don't worry – I've got an idea," said Kirsty. "This door has an old-fashioned lock. It should be just big enough for us to squeeze through."

She flew down to the lock and peered into the keyhole. There was a key on the other side. Kirsty placed her hands on it. "Can you give me a push?" she asked.

Rachel and Catherine pushed, and Kirsty shoved. For a moment, nothing happened. Then there was a loud scraping noise, and the heavy key came out of the lock and fell onto the floor with a loud bang. The little fairies squeezed through the keyhole and found

themselves in a long gallery with a dark
wooden floor. It had been polished so
hard that it shone like a mirror.

"No need to ask where the goblins
are!" said Catherine.

The goblins were making a lot of noise.
The fairies flew along the narrow gallery
and saw the goblins at the end, sliding
along the slippery floor in their bare feet
and shrieking with laughter.

"They shouldn't be in here," said Kirsty.
"The sign on the door said 'No Entry'."

"I think it's because this part isn't finished," said Rachel, pointing to an area that was full of stepladders and dustsheets.

"Let's get closer and make sure they don't get into trouble," said Kirsty. "They're so naughty that they might mess around with the equipment and hurt themselves."

They fluttered overhead, hoping that the goblins wouldn't look up.

"I've got an idea!" shouted the bigger goblin, who had a hairy mole on the tip of his nose. "Let's see how fast the shoe will go!"

He pulled off his backpack and tipped
it upside down. Out fell a half-eaten
apple, a few lumps of mouldy cheese, a
whoopee cushion, a stink bomb and a
tiny shoe that sparkled with miniature
diamonds. It was much too small to fit
any foot.

"Ready, steady, GO!" shouted the
goblin.

He pushed the shoe along the floor as
hard as he could, and it shot along the
long, polished floor so fast that it was just
a blur.

Catherine let out a horrified squeak. "That's my ornamental shoe – and they're going to break it!"

Trapped!

Rachel and Kirsty didn't know what to do, but the second goblin snatched the shoe and hugged it to his chest.

"You shouldn't play with it!" he squawked. "Jack Frost would be cross. We're supposed to be hiding it, not messing around."

The goblin with the mole sniggered.

"You always suck up to Jack Frost," he said. "And I know why. You're a cowardy custard!"

"I am *not* a cowardy custard!" cried the second goblin in an outraged voice.

"Cowardy cowardy custard!" shouted the goblin with the mole.

"Stop saying that!" The second goblin stamped his foot and pulled a horrible face. "I'm going to hide this stupid shoe and go home."

Still squabbling, the goblins stomped off towards the far end of the gallery and the fairies fluttered along overhead.

"What shall we do?" Catherine asked.

"Let's wait," said Kirsty, squeezing the fairy's hand. "The goblins will leave after they hide the shoe. Then we can just take it back without them finding out!"

At the far end of the gallery, the goblins stopped beside a large sculpture in the shape of a vase. It was standing on a pedestal, and it was green on the outside and bright orange on the inside.

"Jack Frost is so clever!" The goblin who was holding the shoe looked up at the sculpture with a soppy smile.

"Those pesky fairies will never think of looking in a place like this."

"There's no point flattering Jack Frost now — he can't hear you," sneered the goblin with the mole. "I bet I could think up a better hiding place."

"Jack Frost has ears everywhere," said the second goblin.

They both glanced around, and then looked at each other.

"Let's just dump the shoe and get out of here," sighed the goblin with the mole.

"I'm bored of listening to all those humans going on about their silly princess."

The second goblin dropped the ornamental shoe into the vase sculpture with an echoing THUNK. As soon as he had let it go, the goblin with the mole pushed him and the second goblin tumbled to the floor.

"You idiot!" he yelled.

"Oops!" the other goblin giggled.

They walked off,

elbowing and pushing each other.
Rachel, Kirsty and Catherine grinned at
each other and flew over to the vase.

Catherine swooped down into it, with

Kirsty behind her. But before Rachel
could follow them in, she heard a furious
yell. The goblins had glanced back and
spotted them!

Shrieking, the goblins sprinted back

towards them. The second goblin leaped
towards the vase and turned it upside
down. Kirsty, Catherine and the shoe
were trapped. The goblin with the mole
started giggling.

Now that she was close to the second goblin, Rachel could see that it was he who had tried to steal the priceless earring. He curled his lip and pressed down on the vase.

"Got you!" he cried in triumph.

"Let them go!" Rachel exclaimed, hovering in front of him.

The goblin glared at her and then gave a toothy grin.

"Oh, it's you!" he said. "This time you're not going to trick me. I'm cleverer than the whole silly lot of you!"

A Clever Question

Rachel took a deep breath. Her heart was pounding, but she knew that it was important not to show the goblin how upset she felt. Her friends were trapped and the royal event might depend on what happened next. She had to stay calm.

"If you're so clever, you should prove it," she said. "I'll ask you one question, and your answer will show how clever you are. Do you agree?"

The goblin looked around for advice, but his goblin companion was still helpless with giggles.

"All right," he said. "What's the question?"

"It's very simple," said Rachel. "Tell me the colour of the inside of the vase."

The goblin gaped at her and then laughed.

"Easy peasy," he said.

106

"It was orange."

Rachel shook her head.

"I think it was blue," she said.

"Stupid fairy, it was orange!" he yelled.

"Prove it," said Rachel. "Otherwise I'll tell all the fairies that you got the question wrong."

The goblin was so angry that his face turned quite yellow.

"Don't you dare!" he squawked. "Look!"

He lifted the vase and held it out to her.

"See?" he said. "Orange! Now who's the clever one?"

"Not *you*!" bawled the goblin with the mole, whose giggles had instantly stopped. "You're letting them escape!"

Catherine and Kirsty zoomed out of

the vase and twirled
high up out of
the goblins'
reach.
Catherine
was
carrying
her
beautiful
sparkling
shoe in her
hand.

"You're the
stupidest goblin ever!" hollered the goblin
with the mole, bashing the second goblin
over the head. "It was all a trick. What
are we going to tell Jack Frost now?"

He grabbed the second goblin by the
scruff of the neck and marched him

away, glowering at the fairies.

Catherine smiled at Rachel as they watched the goblins leave.

"Thank you!" she said. "For a moment I thought we might be stuck inside the vase forever!"

"I would never have let that happen," said Rachel, giving her a hug.

They fluttered to the ground and Catherine waved

her wand. In the blink of an eye, the girls had returned to human size.

"I have to return to Fairyland with the ornamental shoe," she said.

"But what about your final missing object?" Kirsty asked.

"As soon as I hear any news about the jewelled clutch bag, I'll come and find

you," Catherine promised. "But right now, you have a gallery opening to attend!"

With a happy wave, she vanished back to Fairyland. Rachel and Kirsty shared an excited smile, and then half ran, half skidded towards the door. They slipped back into the hall and closed the door behind them.

Then they heard Bee calling them.

"Rachel! Kirsty! Come quickly – the princess has arrived!"

There was an air of hushed excitement in the room as the girls hurried towards Bee.

Just as they reached her side, there was a commotion at the entrance and Princess Edie walked into the gallery. She was wearing a swishy daisy-print dress and a daisy clip in her flicked-out hair. She saw

Bee and waved, smiling at Rachel and
Kirsty. Then she stepped up beside the
little velvet curtain.

"I'm delighted to declare this beautiful
gallery officially open," she said.

She pulled on the tassel and the curtain opened to reveal a plaque.

Grand City Gallery
Opened by Princess Edie

Among the applause, Rachel and Kirsty shared a happy hug.

"I'm so glad that we've found two of Catherine's magical objects," said Rachel.

"Just the jewelled clutch bag to go," said Kirsty. "And I can't wait for the next adventure to start!"

The
Jewelled
Clutch Bag

Contents

A Midnight Visitor

Kirsty woke up with a start. For a few moments she lay still in the darkness, listening. What had disturbed her? Everything seemed quiet. It was the middle of the night, and even her parents and Aunt Bee would be in bed by now.

"Rachel?" she whispered at last. "Are you awake?"

"Yes," Rachel replied at once. "Did you hear that noise?"

"Something woke me up," Kirsty said. "Let's listen carefully."

They waited, and then they heard a tinkling sound like far-off bells. Out of the darkness came a faint golden glow that grew stronger and stronger, until it lit up the room enough that the girls could see each other. Then a golden spark of light darted around the room.

"Is it a firefly?" asked Rachel, rubbing her eyes.

"No, it's getting bigger," said Kirsty. "I think it's magic!"

The girls watched in delight as Catherine the Fashion Princess Fairy appeared in a puff of sparkling fairy dust.

She held up her wand, which glowed with a golden light that lit up the whole room.

"Oh girls, I'm so sorry for waking you in the middle of the night," she said in a breathless voice. "Something has happened that can't wait till tomorrow. You see, Princess Grace is making her speech first thing in the morning, and the jewelled clutch bag is still missing."

"Does that mean it's too late?" asked

Rachel, feeling alarmed.

"Perhaps not," said Catherine. "I've just had a visit from a friendly night owl who told me something very strange. He said that he was flying over the goblin village when he saw a goblin standing on a podium, making a speech."

The girls exchanged a puzzled glance. Goblins usually liked disrupting speeches, not making them!

"Did the owl listen to the speech?" Kirsty asked.

Catherine nodded. "The goblin was

making speeches about anything and everything, and that's what makes me think he might have my jewelled clutch bag. You see, it gives people the confidence to make speeches. Will you come to Goblin Grotto and help me try to get it back?"

"Yes, of course," Rachel said, jumping out of bed.

"We wouldn't let you go to the goblin village by yourself," Kirsty added.

The little fairy perched on the dressing table while the girls

pulled on jeans, T-shirts and jumpers. She glanced down at her elegant green gown.

"I've never been to Goblin Grotto before," she said. "Do you think I should wear something else?"

"We'll need to be disguised if we're going to be hunting for the clutch bag," said Kirsty. "And the goblin village will be cold. I think we all need to be

wrapped up in something warm."

"No sooner said than done," said
Catherine, waving her wand.

A sparkling ribbon of fairy dust coiled
out of the wand and wrapped around
the girls. They looked at themselves
in the mirror and giggled. They were
wearing warm coats, with
thick scarves and
hats pulled down
low. Only their
eyes and noses
could be seen.
Catherine had
a white, fluffy
hat and a long
coat to match.

She waved her
wand, and the dimly

lit bedroom disappeared around them,
as if the walls faded into the night.
Suddenly they were standing in a cold,
deserted street, with stars twinkling above
them and a frosty nip in the air. Goblin
huts were crowded all around. They were
standing in the middle of Goblin Grotto.

Gift of the Gab

Catherine hovered between the girls, shivering as she looked around.

"It's so dismal here," she said.

"The goblins like it," said Rachel. "It's home sweet home for them."

"That's strange," said Kirsty, who was gazing at the huts. "It's the middle of the night, but all the huts still have their lights on."

Suddenly the street was flooded with moonlight. The girls looked up and saw that the moon had slipped out from behind tendrils of wispy clouds. Rachel darted across to the nearest hut, stood on her tiptoes and peered in through the window.

"Empty," she said, turning to Kirsty and Catherine.

Kirsty went to the next hut, but that was empty too. They made their way down the street, peering into the huts as they went. There was not a goblin to be seen, but all the lights were on.

"This is the way to the centre of the village," said Kirsty after a little while. "I remember it from when we came here before."

"Oh yes!" said Rachel, smiling as she remembered. "We came to find Stella the Star Fairy's star decoration."

But when the girls reached the central village square, they stopped in their tracks. The last time they had been here, the square had been filled with grown-up goblins and goblin children, singing carols and eating hot pies. But now it looked very different.

133

The square was still packed with goblins, but they were standing still and – strangest of all – they were completely silent.

A short, plump goblin was standing on a box in the centre of the square. He was towering above the crowd of goblins.

"And another thing," he was saying in a loud voice. "Being green is very

unusual. It isn't like being blue or purple
or red. There are lots of other colours
that are different from the colour green.
There's puce, teal, orange, yellow …"

"Oh my goodness," Rachel whispered.
"What a … wonderful subject for a
speech!"

Catherine gave her a puzzled look.

"Everyone else is fascinated," said
Kirsty. "I've never heard a goblin sound
so interesting."

"He's using magic," said Catherine, frowning. "Look under his arm. He's got my jewelled clutch bag! It gives him the magical power to make speeches that everyone wants to hear."

The goblin finished his speech and the watching goblins burst into loud applause.

"My next subject is cold feet," he announced. "As a special and handsome goblin, most things about me are pretty perfect. But my bare feet are always a bit nippy."

Rachel tried to turn away and found that she couldn't move her feet.

"Put your hands over your ears," Catherine said in an urgent whisper.

The little fairy's ears were covered by her hat, but neither Kirsty nor Rachel could make themselves cover theirs. The speech was so interesting, they couldn't bear to stop listening to the goblin speaking.

"I'm stuck," Kirsty whispered. "I can't walk away."

"STOP!" someone roared.

The goblin flew sideways and disappeared from view. He had been shoved off the box by an angry hand. The clutch bag fell to the ground.

"Oh, I can move again!" said Rachel. "What happened?"

"The goblin isn't holding the bag, so its magic isn't working for him," said Catherine. "We have to see what's happened to it!"

"Let's go to the front and find out," said Kirsty.

Goblins were eagerly leaving the square, so it was hard for the girls to push their way to the front. When they reached the box where the goblin had been standing, they stopped in shock. Jack Frost had the goblin by the scruff of his neck!

Following Jack Frost

Jack Frost was shaking his fist and shouting. Catherine darted out of sight behind Rachel and Kirsty.

"You were supposed to hide that bag, you goose-brained green fool!" Jack Frost was bellowing. "Did I tell you to start making your own speeches? Did I tell

you to think for yourself? No! I told you
to make the Fashion Princess Fairy's job
impossible. I told you to stop Princess
Grace from making another boring royal
fairy speech. I *didn't* say 'please stand on
a box and witter on about cold feet until
you've bored everyone to sleep'."

"They wanted to listen!" the goblin
squawked. "I'm interesting! I'm
intelligent!"

"You're a nincompoop!" Jack Frost
shouted, shaking him.

The clutch bag was still lying on the
floor.

"Perhaps I can grab the bag while
Jack Frost is telling the goblin off," Kirsty
whispered. "Catherine, get ready to
magic us away as soon as I'm holding
the bag."

"I'm ready," said Catherine, holding up her wand. "Good luck, Kirsty!"

Kirsty dashed forward, but just at that moment Jack Frost let go of the goblin, picked up the bag and stormed off in the opposite direction.

"Where's he going?" asked Rachel.

Jack Frost was stomping along a winding path that led upwards to the Ice Castle on the hill. The ice on the path was sparkling in the moonlight.

"He's going home," said Kirsty. "Let's follow him – perhaps if we can catch him up, we can find a way to get the jewelled clutch bag back."

All around them, goblins were still hurrying home, and the crowds were thinning out. All the goblins had their heads down against the bitter wind, so none of them even glanced at the girls and the little fairy.

"Be careful on the path," said
Catherine. "That ice looks very slippery."

The girls hurried after Jack Frost as
quickly as they could, with Catherine
fluttering behind
them. Their feet
slid on the ice
but they kept
going, feeling glad
that they were so well
wrapped up against
the cold weather.
Jack Frost was
skidding on the
ice as well, but
he was too far
ahead for the girls to be able
to catch him up.
He reached the Ice Castle and burst

through the door, scattering goblin
guards as he went.

"How can we get in?" Catherine asked.

"Shall we see if there are any windows
open?"

"It's too dark and cold," said Rachel.
"We need to get inside quickly, and I've
got an idea. We're so wrapped up that I
think we could pass for goblins. Will you
come with me and try?"

"Of course," said Kirsty, slipping her hand into Rachel's hand.

The girls walked up to the Ice Castle with their shoulders pressed together, and Catherine tucked herself in behind them. Rachel knocked on the door and a goblin guard opened it and glared at her.

"It's past bedtime," he snapped. "Why are you still up?"

"We've come to say goodnight to Jack Frost from all the village goblins," said Kirsty. The guard glared at

147

her.

"Your nose doesn't look very green," he said in a suspicious voice.

"It's a very cold night," said Kirsty, thinking quickly. "This is the colour goblin noses go when they're cold."

The guard quickly put his hand over his own nose.

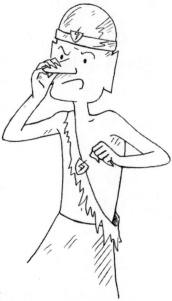

"I don't want that to happen to mine!" he squeaked. "Come in quickly so I can shut the door!"

As soon as they were inside, the goblin guard scurried away, rubbing his nose hard. Catherine gently tapped Rachel and Kirsty with her

wand, and in a flash they felt wings
appear on their backs. Together, they
fluttered up to the ceiling of the entrance
hall. They were inside the castle – but
now they had to find Jack Frost.

The Battle for the Clutch Bag

"Which way now?" asked Catherine, who had never been to the Ice Castle before.

"Let's go to the Throne Room," Rachel suggested in a whisper. "If he's not there, we could try his bedroom. It's in one of the towers."

They flew to the Throne Room, but it was dark and empty. They zoomed up the narrow tower to his bedroom, but that was empty too. They checked all the corridors and flew through chilly halls and echoing chambers, but Jack Frost was nowhere to be seen.

"Where could he be?" Kirsty asked. "He definitely came into the castle."

Suddenly, they heard a sound. It was faint and far away, but they all recognised it.

"That's Jack Frost's voice!" cried Catherine. "Where's it coming from?"

"It's above us," said
Rachel.

She flew over
to the nearest
window and
pushed it open. At
once, the sound of
Jack Frost's voice
grew much louder.

"I think he's outside, at the very top of
the castle," said Rachel. "Come on!"

They swooped out of the window and
upwards to the battlements. Hovering
behind the turrets, they saw Jack Frost
strutting up and down. On either side of
him were rows of goblin guards. They
were all listening to him with their
mouths wide open, and shivering in the
cold night air.

"Of course, everyone knows that I am wonderful and amazing," Jack Frost was saying. "Everyone wants to be me, and I am much more interesting than any silly princess. No one wants to listen to a speech by a princess when they could be listening to me."

He was wearing a thick cloak, and was carrying the jewelled clutch bag.

Catherine waved her wand and gave herself, Rachel and Kirsty a pair of fluffy earmuffs.

"We can't risk falling under the spell of Jack Frost's speech," she said. "While he's holding the bag and making a speech, he's fascinating. Quickly, put these on!"

Rachel beckoned to Kirsty and Catherine, and led them back down the side of the castle until they felt it was safe to remove their earmuffs.

"He's carrying the clutch bag under his arm," she said. "Perhaps if Kirsty and I fly towards the bag and push on it hard enough, it might shoot out the  other side. After all, the goblins won't be able to warn him – they'll be too busy listening to his speech."

"I'll go and stand on his other side and catch it as it shoots out," said Catherine.

They put their earmuffs back on and flew up to the battlements. The goblins had icicles hanging from their noses, but not one of them could tear himself away from Jack Frost's speech.

"And another thing," said the Ice Lord. "Whenever I tell you to hide something from the fairies, you always end up handing it straight over to them. You all need to grow some brains! And that is why I intend to invent a brain tree."

Because of the earmuffs, the fairies couldn't hear each other, so Rachel mouthed the words "Ready, steady, go!" and then she and Kirsty flew towards Jack Frost. But he turned and saw them out of the corner of his eye.

"Fairies!" he yelled.

"Grab them! Stop them!"

The spell broke and the goblins lunged at the fairies. In a flash, Kirsty swooped up above Jack Frost's head.

"Catch me if you can!" she shouted.

Jack Frost stretched his arms up to grab her, and the clutch bag dropped to the ground.

Magic in the Morning

Catherine swooped down and seized the clutch bag before it could touch the stone of the Ice Castle's battlements. Then she zoomed upwards to join Rachel and Kirsty. Panting, the fairies hovered above the battlements and looked down at Jack Frost and his goblins. They were all jumping into the air, stretching as high as they could to try to reach the fairies.

"Give that back!" Jack Frost bellowed.

"It belongs to Catherine," Rachel called down to him.

"And it's coming back to the tower chamber with me," Catherine added.

She waved her wand, leaving a trail of sparkling fairy dust, and then Rachel and Kirsty spun around so fast that they had to close their eyes. When they looked again, they were back in Catherine's tower chamber. Once more they smelled the sweet perfume that hung in the air, and saw the racks of beautiful clothes.

Catherine let out a long sigh of relief and walked over to her dressing table. She opened the third drawer and put the jewelled clutch bag inside.

"Thanks to you both, all three drawers are full again," she said. "The priceless earring, the ornamental shoe and the jewelled clutch bag are back where they belong."

She held out her arms, and Rachel and Kirsty hurried forward to share a hug. Just then, the chamber grew lighter and a shaft of sunlight winked through the window.

"It's dawn," said Rachel. "We've done it – just in time!"

"Princess Grace will look fantastic, arrive on time and give a wonderful speech," said Catherine. "Thank you for everything you've done, girls. Without you, it would have been a disaster."

"It's been fun to help you," said Kirsty. "And thank you for showing us your amazing fashion collection."

"I hope you'll come to visit me and try on some of the clothes one day," smiled Catherine. "But right now I need to help Princess Grace dress for her speech."

"And we should go back to Bee's house and get some sleep," said Rachel, suddenly realising how tired she felt. "Wish the princess good luck from us."

"I will," Catherine said, smiling.

She waved her wand and the girls found themselves back in their pyjamas and tucked into their warm beds. Catherine fluttered above them as they yawned and snuggled into their pillows.

"Goodnight, Rachel and Kirsty," she whispered. "Sweet dreams, and look out for a little surprise when you wake up."

The girls were so tired that they fell asleep even before Catherine disappeared back to Fairyland. They didn't stir until late the next morning.

"Come on, girls, wakey wakey!" called Mr Tate through the bedroom door. "You're wasting sunshine!"

Laughing, Rachel and Kirsty hopped out of bed and started to get dressed. But when Rachel looked in the dressing-table mirror, she got a big surprise.

"Kirsty, look!" she exclaimed.

The mirror was shimmering, like a lake rippling in the breeze.

"It's magic," said Kirsty in a hushed voice.

Slowly the ripples cleared and a picture appeared. Princess Grace was standing among a crowd of smiling fairies.

The girls couldn't hear what she was saying, but they could see that the fairies were listening to every word. They were smiling and it was obvious that the speech was going very well. Catherine the Fashion Princess Fairy was standing nearby, and as the girls watched, she turned and winked at them.

"She must have cast a special spell so we could watch Princess Grace," said Rachel. "I'm so happy that we were able to help her."

"Just like Aunt Bee helps the youngest princess," said Kirsty with a smile. "Perhaps our life isn't so different from theirs after all!"

Now it's time for Kirsty and
Rachel to help...

Alyssa
the Snow Queen Fairy

Read on for a sneak peek...

"What an icy, grey December this is,"
said Rachel Walker, blowing on her
fingers and shivering. "I'm starting to
wonder if Christmas will ever arrive!"

It was Saturday morning, and Rachel
was in her garden with her best friend,
Kirsty Tate. They had come out to play
a game of ball, but the sleet was getting
heavier. Kirsty shivered too, and buried
her hands deep in her pockets.

"I'm really glad to be staying with you
for the weekend, but I wish the weather

wasn't so horrible," she said.

"We had such lovely things planned," said Rachel. "But nature walks and boating on the lake won't be much fun when it's so grey and freezing. It looks as if we'll be spending most of the weekend inside."

"Never mind," said Kirsty, grinning at her friend. "We always have fun when we're together, no matter what we're doing."

"You're right," said Rachel, trying to forget about the dark clouds above.

"Perhaps we should go inside," Kirsty said. "I think it's starting to snow."

"Oh, really?" said Rachel, feeling more cheerful. "Maybe we can go sledging."

"I don't think so," said Kirsty. "I can only see one snowflake."

She pointed up to the single, perfect

snowflake. It was spiralling down from the grey sky. The girls watched it land on the edge of a stone birdbath.

"That's funny," said Rachel after a moment. "It's not melting."

Kirsty took a step closer to the birdbath. "I think it's getting bigger," she said.

The snowflake began to grow bigger and bigger. Then it popped like a snowy balloon and the girls saw a tiny fairy standing in its place. She was as exquisite as the snowflake had been. Her blonde hair flowed around her shoulders, and she was wearing a long blue gown, decorated with sparkling silver sequins. A furry cape was wrapped around her shoulders, and a snowflake tiara twinkled on her head.

"Hello, Rachel and Kirsty," said the fairy. "I'm Alyssa the Snow Queen Fairy."

"Hello, Alyssa!" said Rachel. "It's great

to meet you!"

"What are you doing here in Tippington?" Kirsty asked.

"I've come to ask for your help," said Alyssa in a silvery voice. "It's my job to make sure that everyone stays happy in winter – in both the human and fairy worlds. I went to visit Queen Titania this morning, and when I came home I got a terrible shock. Jack Frost had gone into my home and taken my three magical objects. Without the magical snowflake, the enchanted mirror and the everlasting rose, I can't look after human beings or fairies this winter."

"Oh no, that's awful!" Rachel exclaimed. "Is there any way that we can help you?"

Alyssa clasped her hands together.

"Please, would you come to Fairyland

with me?" she asked. "Queen Titania
has told me so much about you. When
I found that my objects were missing, I
thought of you straight away. Will you
help me to find out what Jack Frost has
done with them?"

Kirsty and Rachel nodded at once.

"Of course we will," Kirsty replied.

"Then let's go!" exclaimed Alyssa,
holding up her wand.

Read **Alyssa the Snow Queen Fairy**
to find out what adventures are in store
for Kirsty and Rachel!

Join in the magic online by signing up
to the Rainbow Magic fan club!

Meet the fairies, play games and
get sneak peeks at the latest books!

There's fairy fun for everyone at

www.rainbowmagicbooks.co.uk

You'll find great activities, competitions, stories and
fairy profiles, and also a special newsletter.

Find a fairy with
your name!